Bookclub-in-a-Box presents the discussion companion for J.M. Coetzee's novel
Disgrace

Published by Vintage 2000, London. First published in Great Britain, 1999, by Martin Secker & Warburg.
ISBN: 0-09-928952-0

Quotations used in this guide have been taken from the text of the paperback edition of **Disgrace**. All information taken from other sources is acknowledged.

This discussion companion for **Disgrace** has been prepared and written by Marilyn Herbert, originator of Bookclub-in-a-Box. Marilyn Herbert. B.Ed., is a teacher, librarian, speaker and writer. Bookclub-in-a-Box is a unique guide to current fiction and classic literature intended for book club discussions, educational study seminars, and personal pleasure. For more information about the Bookclub-in-a-Box team, visit our website.

Bookclub-in-a-Box discussion companion for Disgrace

ISBN 10: 0-9733984-5-0
ISBN 13: 9780973398458

This guide reflects the perspective of the Bookclub-in-a-Box team and is the sole property of Bookclub-in-a-Box.

©2005 BOOKCLUB-IN-A-BOX
©2008 AP EDITION

Unauthorized reproduction of this book or its contents for republication in whole or in part is strictly prohibited.

CONTACT INFORMATION: SEE BACK COVER.

BOOKCLUB-IN-A-BOX
J.M. Coetzee's Disgrace

READERS AND LEADERS GUIDE   2

INTRODUCTION
- Suggested Beginnings 7
- Novel Quickline 9
- Keys to the Novel 10

CHARACTERIZATION
- David Lurie 15
- Lucy, Petrus 16
- Melanie 17
- Soraya 18
- Mr. Isaacs, Ryan, Pollux ... 19
- Bev & Bill Shaw 20
- Rosalind 21

FOCUS POINTS / THEMES
- Power 25
- Illusion of Power 26
- Abuse of Power 28
  - boundaries 29
  - rape 30
  - loss 32
- Shift of Power 32
- New Balance 35

WRITING STYLE / STRUCTURE
- Narration 41
- Language 42
- Parallels/Juxtapositions 46

SYMBOLS
- Grace, Disgrace 51
- South Africa 54
- Dante 58
- Dogs 58
- Opera 60

LAST THOUGHTS
- Literary/Historical Allusion . 65
- Lord Byron, Teresa 67

HISTORICAL REFERENCE
- Apartheid 71
- ANC 72
- Truth & Reconciliation Commission 72
- Population/Demographics ..74

AUTHOR INFORMATION 79

FROM THE NOVEL (QUOTES) .. 85

ACKNOWLEDGEMENTS 93

BOOKCLUB-IN-A-BOX

Readers and Leaders Guide

Each Bookclub-in-a-Box guide is clearly and effectively organized to give you information and ideas for a lively discussion, as well as to present the major highlights of the novel. The format, with a Table of Contents, allows you to pick and choose the specific points you wish to talk about. It does not have to be used in any prescribed order. In fact, it is meant to support, not determine, your discussion.

You Choose What to Use.

You may find that some information is repeated in more than one section and may be cross-referenced so as to provide insight on the same idea from different angles.

The guide is formatted to give you extra space to make your own notes.

How to Begin

Relax and look forward to enjoying your bookclub.

With Bookclub-in-a-Box as your behind the scenes support, there is little for you to do in the way of preparation.

Some readers like to review the guide after reading the novel; some before. Either way, the guide is all you will need as a companion for your discussion. You may find that the guide's interpretation, information, and background have sparked other ideas not included.

Having read the novel and armed with Bookclub-in-a-Box, you will be well prepared to lead or guide or listen to the discussion at hand.

Lastly, if you need some more 'hands-on' support, feel free to contact us. (See Contact Information)

What to Look For

Each Bookclub-in-a-Box guide is divided into easy-to-use sections, which include points on characters, themes, writing style and structure, literary or historical background, author information, and other pertinent features unique to the novel being discussed. These may vary slightly from guide to guide.

INTERPRETATION OF EACH NOVEL REFLECTS THE PERSPECTIVE OF THE BOOKCLUB-IN-A-BOX TEAM.

Do We Need to Agree?

THE ANSWER TO THIS QUESTION IS NO.

If we have sparked a discussion or a debate on certain points, then we are happy. We invite you to share your group's alternative findings and experiences with us. You can respond on-line at our website or contact us through our Contact Information. We would love to hear from you.

Discussion Starters

There are as many ways to begin a bookclub discussion as there are members in your group. If you are an experienced group, you will already have your favorite ways to begin. If you are a newly formed group or a group looking for new ideas, here are some suggestions.

Ask for people's impressions of the novel. (This will give you some idea about which parts of the unit to focus on.)

- Identify a favorite or major character.
- Identify a favorite or major idea.
- Begin with a powerful or pertinent quote. (not necessarily from the novel)
- Discuss the historical information of the novel. (not applicable to all novels)
- If this author is familiar to the group, discuss the range of his/her work and where this novel stands in that range.
- Use the discussion topics and questions in the Bookclub-in-a-Box guide.

If you have further suggestions for discussion starters, be sure to share them with us and we will share them with others.

Above All, Enjoy Yourselves

INTRODUCTION

Suggested Beginnings

Novel Quickline

Keys to the Novel

INTRODUCTION

Suggested Beginnings

1. David Lurie and the three black men who attacked Lucy are representatives of the two sides of abuse of power in South Africa.

Is it possible to sympathize with either side as they are presented here?

2. Coetzee, the master linguist, shows his talents in the novel.

Pick any passage in the novel and see what word references, allusions, double entendres, and alternative pictures Coetzee creates.

3. At first glance, this novel is deceptively simple.

Considering Coetzee's extensive and complex use of language, is it still possible to consider this book a "simple" one? How does the narrative style influence the reader's appreciation of the novel?

4. Like the Teresa of Lurie's imagination, there is a new South Africa: imperfect by some standards, and unloved by others.

Consider how the character Teresa can be a symbol for South Africa.

5. In the novel, David Lurie is seen as extremely resistant to change and seems to be content with the status quo of his life. Although many whites participated in changing the situation, others were happy for things to remain as they were.

Consider Lurie's position with respect to the white community of that time in South Africa.-

6. Lucy has legal title to the land she owns. In selling to Petrus, she is trading title for protection.

Should she be forced to give up her land? Considering post-apartheid events, could a 'better deal' have been made then? Now?

7. The attacks on Lucy and Melanie involve both their families (Lucy and her father, David Lurie; Melanie together with her father, mother, sister and boyfriend).

Is Coetzee alluding to all of South Africa as a family and is he, therefore, saying that if one member (black or white) endures injustice, the whole country suffers?

8. Lurie treats the university committee's investigation of his "crime" with disdain and "subtle mockery."

Why does he do this? What does this say about authority?

9. In the novel, Coetzee presents and discusses abuse through improper use of authority as it pertains to women, race, and animals.

Consider Coetzee's point of view and whether you agree with it.

10. Rosalind, Lurie's ex-wife, is an objective voice pointing out to Lurie the obvious discrepancies between his actions and his values.

Whose opinion is Rosalind representing? The outside world's? Coetzee's?

11. Petrus was nowhere to be found before and during the attack on Lucy.

How much did he know about the events? Was his inaction simply vengeance against perceived past injustices?

12. The process for overcoming disastrous personal events is very difficult. **How does a nation (South Africa) and its communities overcome a tragic and debilitating history? Is it possible to parallel these two ideas? What comes next? Is it necessary to assign blame in order to move on?**

13. If you know anyone from South Africa, invite this person to your discussion. Personal stories will add an interesting dimension. Alternatively, if anyone in your group has read any other books about South Africa, it would be interesting to compare or contrast **Disgrace** with those works.

Novel Quickline

David Lurie, teacher, father, writer, twice-divorced and currently single, has committed a disgraceful act: he has seduced a student in his Communications class at Cape Technical University, and he has done so, by all appearances, against her will.

A harassment complaint is issued against him. Although the university gives Lurie an opportunity to put this incident behind him and to carry on in his position, Lurie simply does not act on it.

Lurie rashly leaves his job and his home and goes to stay temporarily with his daughter, who owns a small farm in eastern South Africa. She is living a simple and solitary life, raising some crops and boarding dogs. At the farm, as Lurie tries to figure out where his life should next go, a second abrupt incident throws not only his life but his understanding of it into turmoil.

Nothing is as simple as it seems. Each word and sentence has been calculated to create a subtle impact. There are many layers of understanding and meaning to this small but powerful novel.

Keys to the Novel

Illusion, Appearance

- The truth of a situation or an event must be considered through the perspective of the participants. Because a single perspective can still be illusory, Coetzee presents multiple points of view through several stories, each of which is simply an enlargement of the one before.
(see Parallels, p.46)

- He starts with the simple relationship of Lurie and Soraya. The illusion, for both the reader and for Lurie, is that Soraya is under Lurie's control: he pays, she appears, they have sex – a simple arrangement. As we find out within a few pages, the reality of the relationship is quite different. Lurie is anything but in control.

- Coetzee then takes us through the parallel stories of the novel's other female characters: Melanie, Lucy, and even Byron's Teresa. He shows the dual nature of how these relationships present themselves.

- Coetzee's goal is to bring the reader to the realization that each of these relationships is a microcosm of the complex relationships that exist within the population of South Africa, especially between whites and blacks.

Power   *Boundaries, Change, Balance*

- Successful relationships depend upon an acceptance of where the boundaries of those relationships are drawn. When the boundaries in the novel are crossed, chaos sets in with increasing cost each time.

- When Lurie crosses the boundary Soraya has set, he loses a minor sexual relationship. When Lurie crosses the more important student-teacher boundary with Melanie, he loses his job and his way of life. When Lucy is raped, the "boundaries" of her person and her way of life are brutally violated.

- Coetzee is talking about the artificial boundary that had previously existed through apartheid. He is looking at how the blacks and whites are each presently crossing that boundary, and how the new realignment between the communities might look in the future. The illusion of the workability of the old boundaries has been exposed and broken. *"Then one day, it all ended."* (p.7) In **Disgrace**, this is where the story begins.

Grace, Disgrace

- The concepts of grace/disgrace must be viewed together. Grace is based on the ideas of *"elegance or beauty of form ... a manifestation of favor, especially by a superior ... mercy, clemency or pardon ... favor shown in granting a delay or temporary immunity ... the condition of being in God's favor or the condition of being one of the elect."* (Random House Dictionary) Coetzee uses the idea of grace in all its meanings.

- Disgrace is the absence of all of the above and adds the idea of *"shame ... dishonor [and] exclusion from confidence or trust."* (Random House)

- Coetzee does not bring the stories of Lurie and Lucy to a close, but to a point where he feels they can each begin anew. There are no comfortable solutions, but they have each achieved a sense of grace through the acknowledgement, acceptance, and understanding of the new reality of their lives. Perhaps that is the only solution for their future and for their country.

CHARACTERIZATION

David Lurie

Lucy, Petrus

Melanie

Soraya

Mr. Isaacs

Ryan

Pollux

Bev & Bill Shaw

Rosalind

CHARACTERIZATION

David Lurie, Lucy, Petrus, Melanie, Soraya, Mr. Isaacs, Ryan (Melanie's boyfriend), Pollux, Bill and Bev Shaw, Rosalind.

David Lurie

- Lurie appears to be, but is not, a simple character. As a former professor of modern languages, he appears to have the ability to communicate successfully on many levels. But even before the novel opens, we find that his position has been reduced to the teaching of first-year Romantics and Communications. He teaches the romantic poets but is not at all a romantic person, and he teaches communication, but in reality, he cannot make meaningful contact with anyone.

- Lurie has intellectual arrogance but no integrity. He pleads guilty to sexual harassment of Melanie but gives no explanation and, at that time, offers no sincere apology.

Lucy

- Lucy, David's daughter, is a single, mature woman, who lives alone on a farm and *"makes a living: from the kennels, and from selling flowers and garden produce. Nothing could be more simple."* (p.61)

- On one hand, as a rape victim, Lucy symbolizes the South Africa that has been raped by the segregationist policies of the white leadership of the apartheid era. On the other hand, she represents the current situation, which includes attacks by blacks on the remaining white population. Lucy brings us (and Lurie) to understand that there is a price to pay for South Africa's history. Through Lucy, Coetzee shows that the issue for South Africa is not simply one of vengeance but one of abrupt and violent change, revealing the impact of decades of oppression by one group on another. (see Historical Reference, p.71)

   What if ... what if that is the price one has to pay for staying on? Perhaps that is how they look at it; perhaps that is how I should look at it too. They see me as owing something. They see themselves as debt collectors, tax collectors. Why should I be allowed to live here without paying? (p.158)

Petrus

- Petrus, Lucy's gardener and dog man, new landowner, and entrepreneur, is a symbol of the emergence of the new order in South Africa. Lurie finds Petrus sitting beside him on the couch watching soccer, holding *"a bottle of beer in his hand."* (p.75) Lucy tells Lurie that *"Petrus is busy establishing his own lands"* (p.76) and asks Lurie to give Petrus a hand.

- This is a clear example of role reversal. Lurie, the once powerful and prominent professor, is reduced to being a helping hand to Lucy and her hired man. Lurie asks sarcastically, *"Will he pay me a wage for my labour, do you think?"* but Lucy's response is not at all sarcastic. *"Ask him. I'm sure he will."* (p.77)

- Petrus is an enigma, because the reader is not really sure about the nature of his relationship with Lucy. They seem to co-exist peacefully and to have a mutually beneficial relationship. Although Petrus owns his own land, he still helps Lucy. Lucy has installed electricity on his farm. But there are hints early in the novel that this situation may not be as simple or as comfortable as it seems.

    "Yes," says Petrus, "it is dangerous." He pauses. "Everything is dangerous today. But here it is all right, I think." And he gives another smile. (p.64)

Melanie

- Melanie, the young, innocent, Asian student, is compromised by David Lurie for his own pleasure. She is a passive victim, who feels she has no power to resist the older, authoritative professor.

- *"Melanie; the dark one"* (p.18) is more than likely of East Indian descent. (see Population, p.74) She has *"close-cropped black hair, wide, almost Chinese cheekbones, [and] large, dark eyes."* (p.11) Had she been white like Amanda, the *"wispy blonde"* (p.29), Lurie wouldn't have been interested. Had she been black, Lurie couldn't have been interested. South Africa may be changing, but it is not yet that different. Melanie is neither white nor black, allowing Lurie to wield power without breaking a taboo.

- Like Lucy, Melanie is another symbol of South Africa. Although Melanie is overpowered by Lurie, she is not defeated; later, Lucy is overpowered by Pollux but not crushed. Melanie rises and, with the help of her family and her boyfriend, Ryan, she defeats Lurie. He loses his job and his life as he has known it up to then.

Soraya

- Soraya, Lurie's paid mistress, is, like Melanie, of Asian background. Soraya is *"tall and slim, with long black hair and dark, liquid eyes ..."* (p.1) Her body is honey-brown. Again, like Melanie, Soraya is a safe middle ground in this country weighed down with racial anxiety. However, she is a double-edged sword because she leads two contradictory lives: one as a respectable wife and mother; the other as a prostitute.

- Soraya has compartmentalized the two sides of her life. A parallel is drawn to South Africa under apartheid. Lurie tries to cross the line into Soraya's private life and, in doing so, violates the boundaries and upsets the balance of their relationship. Separation is successful only as long as everyone stays on their side of the line. There is to be no mixing or crossing over.

    > *That was how he [David, South Africa] lived; for years, for decades, that was the backbone of his life.* (p.7)
    > (see Illusion of Power, p.26)

- For Lurie and Soraya, as for South Africa, *"one day it all ended. Without warning his powers fled."* (p.7) Within ten pages, Soraya is gone and we know that something bad is going to happen.

Mr. Isaacs *Melanie's Father*

- As a father, Mr. Isaacs is duty bound to protect his daughter's honor. (see Boundaries, p.29) As readers, we are shocked to hear him invite Lurie to dinner instead of taking him to task. However, it is Isaacs who shows that vengeance is a less desirable goal than apology. Nothing can come after vengeance except more vengeance. But, after apology, positive action may be possible.

    "So," says Isaacs, "at last you have apologized ... The question is not, are we sorry? The question is, what lesson have we learned? The question is, what are we going to do now that we are sorry?" (p.172)

Ryan *Melanie's Boyfriend*

- Melanie's boyfriend, Ryan, is a member of a new generation, one that doesn't grant unearned respect and doesn't take lightly the abuse of power. He has no patience for pretense but gets right to the point: *"... don't think you can just walk into people's lives and walk out again when it suits you."* (p.30)

- In contrast to Melanie's father, Ryan's protection is active and direct. He backs up his words explicitly. When Lurie's parked car is vandalized, no one has to ask who is responsible.

Pollux

- Of Lucy's three attackers, Pollux is the one presumed to be the father of her unborn child. These men were not just random wanderers but in fact were known to Petrus. Pollux turns out to be a nephew of Petrus's wife and is, as Petrus says, *"my family, my people."* (p.201)

Thus the disparity between the different people of the land is made clear, a definite case of us vs. them – blacks vs. whites.

Bev and Bill Shaw

- The Shaws are Lucy's neighbors and long-time residents of the area where Lucy lives. Bill, who works in a hardware store, was born within two hundred kilometers of where he currently resides. Bev runs the Animal Welfare clinic as a volunteer and acts as its unofficial vet. She looks after the animals as best as she can and when they are no longer wanted or cared for, Bev helps them to die with dignity. (see Grace, Disgrace, p. 51)

- Through his work with Bev, Lurie begins to move forward to a new level of consciousness and an awareness of the needs and desires of others.

    > At the door Bev presses herself against him a last time, rests her head on his chest. He lets her do it, as he has let her do everything she has felt a need to do ... Well, let poor Bev Shaw go home ... And let him stop calling her poor Bev Shaw. If she is poor, he is bankrupt.
    > (p.150)

- He begins to understand that he can learn new things from the unlikeliest people. Bill's small act of kindness when he picks up Lurie from the hospital is something that Lurie has never before encountered.

    > [Bill Shaw says,] "Nonsense! ... What else are friends for? You would have done the same."
    >
    > Spoken without irony, the words stay with [Lurie] and will not go away. Bill Shaw believes that if he, Bill Shaw, had been hit over the head and set on fire, then

> he, David Lurie, would have driven to the hospital and sat waiting, without so much as a newspaper to read, to fetch him home. Bill Shaw believes that, because he and David Lurie once had a cup of tea together, David Lurie is his friend and the two of them have obligations towards each other. Is Bill Shaw wrong or right? (p.102)

Rosalind

- Rosalind, Lurie's second ex-wife, makes brief but important appearances as Coetzee's objective observer of David Lurie. There doesn't seem to be any significant animosity between her and Lurie. Rosalind stands alone as an honest commentator, and even though she may appear unsympathetic, she is, for Lurie, "*someone to count on when the worst arrives ...*"

   > People talk, David. Everyone knows about this latest affair of yours, in the juiciest detail. It's in no one's interest to hush it up, no one's but your own. Am I allowed to tell you how stupid it looks? (p.43)

- Rosalind tells it like it is.

   > I heard the story of your trial ... I heard you didn't perform well ... trials are not about principles, they are about how well you put yourself across. According to my source, you came across badly. What was the principle you were standing up for?"
   >
   > Freedom of speech. Freedom to remain silent. (p.188)

FOCUS POINTS AND THEMES

Illusion of Power

Abuse of Power

Boundaries

Rape

Loss

Shift of Power

New Balance

FOCUS POINTS AND THEMES

Power

The single overriding theme in **Disgrace** is the topic of power, which includes several subdivisions that follow in a natural progression: the illusions and abuse of power, the shift of who is in control of that power, and the need to establish a workable new balance for everyone. Coetzee is addressing South Africa through the different kinds of real or illusory power that his characters use, as well as through the powers of lust, love, anger, and control that they experience.

Illusion of Power

- Illusion plays a big part in David Lurie's world. Overcoming illusion requires a recognition and an acceptance of the power being wielded, along with a sense of its boundaries. Lurie doesn't see himself as others see him, and he certainly doesn't see a need to change. But Rosalind sees through him.

  > *... you were always a great self-deceiver, David. A great deceiver and a great self-deceiver ... You have thrown away your life, and for what?* (p.188)

- As a professor, he thinks he has the security of status and power, but this is easily lost through his encounter with Melanie. As a single man, he thinks he has the ability to easily attract women into a sexual relationship, but he eventually resorts to hiring a woman to satisfy his sexual desires. Bev Shaw is physically unattractive, but despite her appearance, she is the one person who actually opens Lurie to the possibility of change.

  > *Her hair is a mass of little curls ... The veins on her ears are visible as a filigree of red and purple. The veins of her nose too. And then a chin that comes straight out of her chest, like a pouter pigeon's. As an ensemble, remarkably unattractive.* (p.81, 82)

  Against all probability, Lurie does what was previously unthinkable: he has sex with her. By extension, what was previously unthinkable for South Africa might one day be possible too.

- The first step to dispelling an illusion is to acknowledge that there is a problem. Coetzee knows there is a problem; David Lurie does not.

  > *For a man of his age, fifty-two, divorced, he has, to his mind, solved the problem of sex rather well.* (p.1)

In fact, Lurie has not solved the "sex" problem at all. While Soraya is a paid sexual partner, Lurie deludes himself into thinking that there is a reciprocal affection between the two of them. He is right only up to a point. Lurie's illusions about his relationship with Soraya lightly cover the fact that there are strict boundaries under which the two of them can operate.

> *For an instant through the glass, Soraya's eyes meet his.... this glance between himself and Soraya he regrets at once.* (p.6)

When Lurie tries to cross the boundaries, the delicate balance they have set up crashes. *"Though Soraya still keeps her appointments, he feels a growing coolness as she transforms herself into just another woman and him into just another client."* (p.7)

- The same thing happens with Melanie, only this time Lurie adds to the relationship the element of abuse of position. At no time does he acknowledge the responsibility of his position in either of these relationships. *"He has no wish to upset what must be ... He is all for double lives, triple lives, lives lived in compartments."* (p.6)

- Lurie is invited to a hearing, where charges of keeping false records and charges of harassment are made against him by the school and by Melanie. Lurie pleads guilty but doesn't accept responsibility for either charge.

> *... he is going into this in the wrong spirit. But he does not care.*
> *"That is the sum of it? Those are the charges?"*
> *"They are."*
> *He takes a deep breath. "I am sure the members of this committee have better things to do with their time than rehash a story over which there will be no dispute. I plead guilty to both charges. Pass sentence, and let us get on with our lives."* (p.47, 48)

- Lurie is still under the illusion that life will continue as before, because that is how he has always known it: lay blame, then take up where you have left off. There can be no real change because there is no real acceptance of responsibility by anyone. Even the committee that hears Melanie's complaint has only powers of recommendation, not enforcement. (see Truth and Reconciliation, p.72) The entire event is a *"subtle mockery."* (p.50) In this way, David Lurie is representative of a wider community wish to maintain a status quo.

- Lurie's refusal to accept accountability for his actions continues even as the incidents escalate: until the rape of Lucy. It is only then that Lurie begins to understand something new about his situation.

    A flurry of anger runs through him, strong enough to take him by surprise ... Violation: that is the word he would like to force out of Petrus. Yes, it was a violation, he would like to hear Petrus say; yes, it was an outrage. (p.119)

Abuse of Power

- The understanding that everyone has the right to live without oppression or abuse is only possible when those in power behave responsibly toward those without control. When power is abused, personal boundaries are crossed. In his relationships with both Soraya and Melanie, Lurie deludes himself by thinking it is his right to cross those boundaries, and it is from this belief that he derives his illusion of power. Coetzee presents these situations, each of which illustrates an increasing degree of abuse, ending with the brutal attack on Lucy.

- Lucy's rape is the ultimate consequence of the crossing of boundaries. An analogy can be made to South Africa, where the system of apartheid created a formal separation of the races. Like Lurie, the white community acted on the assumption that it had the right to enforce or cross this boundary as it saw fit. It is this illusion that becomes broken and changed.

Boundaries

- Lurie and Soraya have an unspoken agreement to meet only on neutral ground, a flat owned by Discreet Escorts. (p.2) However, when he sees Soraya with her children, Lurie is tempted by curiosity and a mistaken belief that they share a real affection, but his illusion is solidly shattered.

- As a teacher, Lurie should know to keep his distance from Melanie. The boundary between student and teacher is the classroom door. On one level he understands he should not continue this relationship, but his desire knows no bounds and so he presses forward. Lurie violates the teacher-student boundary when he violates Melanie. *"He is mildly smitten with her. It is no great matter: barely a term passes when he does not fall for one or other of his charges."* (p.12)

- It is not until the attack and rape of Lucy that Lurie begins to understand that he had missed the opportunity to behave responsibly with Melanie. It is not until after the attack on himself and Lucy that Lurie suffers from a sense of having failed Lucy and in the same way had failed Melanie. *"He has had a vision: Lucy has spoken to him; her words – 'Come to me, save me!' – still echo in his ears."* (p.103)

- It is Bev Shaw who leads Lurie to an understanding of what Lucy endured at the hands of her attacker, and Lurie sadly comes to the conclusion that he no longer has, and perhaps never had, the power to protect his daughter. *"Lucy says I can't go on being a father forever. I can't imagine, in this life, not being Lucy's father.'"* (p.162)

- It is immediately after this realization that Lurie goes to see Mr. Isaacs to apologize. Lurie is just beginning to acknowledge and accept his actions, but his actual acceptance of responsibility doesn't come until the very end of the novel.

Rape

- Coetzee gives us the sexual stories of four women: Soraya, Melanie, Lucy, and Teresa. For two of these women, Melanie and Lucy, sex was undesired and forced: they were raped. For each, the act of rape crossed a line that should have protected them. Melanie thought she would be safely respected by her teacher; Lucy thought she would be safely protected by the presence of her dogs.

- As he does with other things and people in the novel, Coetzee parallels the experiences of Melanie and Lucy (see Parallels, p.46), but each successive experience or incident becomes stronger and is more powerful in its depiction. Lurie's violation of Melanie foreshadows the later, more horrible violation of Lucy.

- Melanie is younger than Lucy, young enough to be Lurie's daughter. In fact, he has sex with her for the last time on his daughter's bed. (p.29)

   He has given her no warning; she is too surprised to resist the intruder who thrusts himself upon her. When he takes her in his arms, her limbs crumple like a marionette's. (p.24)

> *Not rape, not quite that, but undesired nevertheless, undesired to the core. As though she had decided to go slack, die within herself for the duration ... So that everything done to her might be done, as it were, far away.* (p.25)

- While both women suffer many of the classic symptoms of rape victims, their individual reactions to their attacks are quite different. While it is not surprising that Melanie eventually lays charges against Lurie, it is Lucy's perspective that catches us breathlessly off guard. She takes her reaction out of the realm of a simple and direct crime and adds a new, complex dimension to it.

  > *Maybe, for men, hating the woman makes sex more exciting. You (Lurie) are a man, you ought to know. When you have sex with someone strange – when you trap her, hold her down, get her under you, put all your weight on her – isn't it a bit like killing? Pushing the knife in; exiting afterwards, leaving the body behind covered in blood – doesn't it feel like murder, like getting away with murder?* (p.158)

- We are never given a detailed account of the attack on Lucy. Instead, Lucy's graphic portrayal of rape as murder is vividly described later through Coetzee's account of the brutal attack on Lucy's dogs. (see Parallels, p.46; Dogs, p.58)

- Both Lucy and Melanie can be seen as symbols of South Africa. The abuse of power against both women is a fact. Although Melanie is overpowered by Lurie, she is not defeated; Lucy is overpowered by Pollux but is not crushed. Clearly power has been abused in South Africa; whether South Africa will overcome it remains to be seen. (see South Africa, p.54)

Loss

Things have been taken: his shoes, his jacket, and that is only the beginning of it. (p.97)

- This quote refers to the attack on Lurie, but everyone in the novel loses something. Melanie loses her innocence; Lucy's sense of self is changed by the rape – she loses her land and her social position; Lurie loses his job, his reputation and his life as an academic; the dogs lose their lives. Lurie comments that this type of violent, aggressive loss *"... happens every day, every hour, every minute, he tells himself, in every quarter of the country."* (p.98)

- With these points, Coetzee refers to the concept of loss, for both blacks and whites, as a consequence of the abuse of power. He is subtly making accusations in all directions because he realizes the enormous cost to the country and to everyone's sense of humanity.

    The events (of the attack) have shocked (Lurie) to the depths ... He has a sense that, inside him, a vital organ has been bruised, abused – perhaps even his heart. For the first time he has a taste of what it will be like to be an old man, tired to the bone, without hopes, without desires, indifferent to the future ... It may take weeks, it may take months before he is bled dry, but he is bleeding ... His pleasure in living has been snuffed out. (p.107)

The Shift of Power *Changes, Role Reversal, A New Idea for South Africa*

- While Lurie is busy with his illusions – who he is and what he can do – the landscape is shifting underneath his feet.

    Then one day it all ended. (p.7)

- At first, it is only Lurie's relationship with Soraya that ends. Next, he knows he ought to end his relationship with Melanie, *"but he does not."* (p.18) When this action results in charges against him, he still does not acknowledge that the status quo is being challenged and the accepted boundaries are being pushed.

    "You charged me, and I pleaded guilty to the charges. That is all you need from me." (Lurie)
    "No. We want more. Not a great deal more, but more." (p.58)

- Lurie refuses to accept the committee's terms of employment and leaves to join Lucy at her farm. Here, at least, change appears to be slower and things appear to be normal.

    [Lucy] ... talks easily about these matters. A frontier farmer of the new breed. In the old days, cattle and maize. Today, dogs and daffodils. The more things change the more they remain the same. History repeating itself, though in a more modest vein. Perhaps history has learned a lesson. (p.62)

- But Lurie finds that even on the farm, things are changing and reversing themselves. He first finds Petrus, the hired man, making himself at home in Lucy's living room. He next finds himself in the position of helping hand to Petrus at the market and in the field. (see Petrus, p.16) Lurie is now the "hired" hand.

- The situation becomes abnormal when Lucy and Lurie are attacked. For a long time, Lurie was oblivious to the fact that things have changed, but now he begins to see it.

    Is this how it is all going to end? ... Who would have thought it! A day like any other day, clear skies, a mild sun, yet suddenly everything is changed, utterly changed! Standing against the wall outside the kitchen, hiding his face in his hands, he heaves and heaves and finally cries. (p.199)

- Throughout the novel, Coetzee declares that changes must be made first by the individual (Lurie), and then by the country. The message is adapt or leave.

    It is a new world they live in, he and Lucy and Petrus. Petrus knows it, and he knows it, and Petrus knows that he knows it ... Petrus has a vision of the future in which people like Lucy have no place. (p.117, 118)

- But change is difficult for everyone. The boundaries have changed, and Lurie finds this change hard to accept.

    Too close, he thinks: we live too close to Petrus. It is like sharing a house with strangers, sharing noises, sharing smells. (p.127)

- In the midst of these changes, Lurie worries for Lucy, who like other whites in South Africa, has chosen to stay amidst a changing social order. (see Historical Reference, p.71)

    As a woman alone on a farm she has no future, that is clear ... If Lucy has any sense she will quit before a fate befalls her worse than death. But of course she will not. She is stubborn, and immersed, too, in the life she has chosen. (p.134)

- Lucy defends her decision to stay:

    Yes, the road I am following may be the wrong one. But if I leave the farm now I will leave defeated, and will taste that defeat for the rest of my life." (p.161)

A New Balance *The Apology and After, Protection, A New State of Balance*

- It takes David Lurie a long time to understand the difference between admitting he has done something wrong and apologizing for it.

    "I have admitted that. Freely. I am guilty of the charges brought against me." (Lurie)

    "Don't play games with us, David. There is a difference between pleading guilty to a charge and admitting you were wrong, and you know that." (see Truth and Reconciliation, p.72)

- His difficulty is accepting the fact that his actions have had undesirable consequences, but when the shoe is on the other foot and his Lucy has been attacked, he doesn't care about anything except finding the attacker and demanding an apology.

    With careful ceremony he gets to his knees and touches his forehead to the floor.

    Is that enough? he thinks. Will that do? If not, what more? (p.173)

- The "what" that is to come after the apology is the public acknowledgement and action that will begin the process of healing. The committee that attempts to hear Lurie's initial charges is modeled after South Africa's Truth and Reconciliation Committee (see Illusion of Power, p.26), which was headed by Bishop Desmond Tutu. (Note that the university committee has a member named Desmond.)

- Neither committee is empowered to bring criminal or even civil charges against an accused; but one of the primary purposes of these committees is to bring to public record a distinct admission of past wrongdoings, to clear the air in order to begin again.

> *The criterion is not whether you [Lurie] are sincere. That is a matter ... for your own conscience. The criterion is whether you are prepared to acknowledge your fault in a public manner and take steps to remedy it."* (p.58)

- What needs to be restored is a new sense of balance for Lurie, Lucy, for South Africa. Everyone's roles have been thrown into chaos and need to be clearly redefined and re-established. This is most true for Lucy. Without Petrus, Lucy would be very vulnerable, *"fair game"* (p.203), in the new order of things. Lucy wants to stay on the land but is pregnant and can only remain under Petrus's protection.

- Petrus is now the new master. However, the new order is not so clear-cut. Petrus is also protecting Pollux, his wife's brother. *"He is a child. He is my family, my people."* (p.201) So Petrus is now in the position of not only protecting Pollux, but in addition, Lucy and her unborn child.

- He offers to marry Lucy and by doing so creates an alliance with her. Lucy will *"contribute the land, in return for which [she is] allowed to creep in under his wing."* (p.203)

- A marriage between two communities: not a mutually desirable one, but a marriage of necessity.

    This is how it begins. (p.38)

- It has taken a cataclysmic event in Lurie's life to get him started on the road to change. Before, it was simply his behavior that was unstoppable. It *"... is his temperament. His temperament is not going to change, he is too old for that. His temperament is fixed, set. The skull, followed by the temperament: the two hardest parts of the body."* (p.2) But Lurie discovers that it is change in the country that is unstoppable.

- The analogy to South Africa's changing society is clear. When Lurie is first charged with misconduct against a student, he offers no defense because he doesn't recognize the legitimacy of the accusatory council. The council offers him a leave of absence and a chance to issue a public statement. Lurie rails futilely against the injustice of this solution. Perhaps, like the South African white community, he feels he is being circled by *"hunters who have cornered a strange beast and do not know how to finish it off."* (p.56)
- Working side by side with Petrus in the field of Lucy's farm, Lurie says to him, *"You know. You know the future. What can I say to that? You have spoken. Do you need me here any longer?"* (p.139)
- Coetzee is asking whether the whites will have a role in the future of a new black-controlled South Africa. Furthermore, the question is not whether whites will want to stay, but the question is how will they leave, in what state of ignominy or disgrace. Like Lurie's opera, *"It has dried up, the source of everything."* (p.183)
- While Coetzee is hesitantly optimistic about South Africa's future, he clearly lays the responsibility for feasible change on the white community. Like Lurie, the community must also make public statements acknowledging responsibility for the history of its actions in the country, and the white community must begin to work side by side with the black community in order to effect significant change. It must go back to the beginning and make the offer of change *"as if [they] were ... visitor[s]. Good. Visitorship, visitation: a new footing, a new start."* (p.218)
- Coetzee acknowledges that this is a difficult sacrifice. In the last words of the novel, Lurie points out that even when you love something fiercely (South Africa), you may have to give it up unselfishly. As a parallel, Lurie can no longer delay giving the young dog he has grown to love the chance for a graceful and natural end to life, one accompanied by his affection and respect. Delay just creates more pain. The end is inevitable; his act is his gift.

> *"I thought you would save him for another week," says Bev Shaw. "Are you giving him up?*
>
> *"Yes, I am giving him up."* (p.220)
>
> *He does not care how he gets the words out of Petrus now, he just wants to hear them.* (p.119)

- To Lurie's credit, and this may be the only thing to his credit, he eventually goes to see Mr. Isaacs and offers an apology. He finally understands that he is being punished for his behavior toward Melanie and that he must change. But even at this profound point, he still doesn't see what is to come after the apology.

WRITING STYLE AND STRUCTURE

Narration

Language

Parallels & Juxtapositions

WRITING STYLE AND STRUCTURE

Narration *Simplicity of the Narrative Style*

- The narrator in **Disgrace** is an objective third person. The telling of this black-and-white tale seems to be plain and easy to understand, but Coetzee's frequent use of the word "simple" brings attention to the fact that things are anything but.

- Looks are deceiving, and the simplicity of the narration illustrates that we should not be deceived by how simple things may appear. It is the structure of the novel and the use of parallels and juxtaposition that underscore how complex this small book is. Coetzee emphasizes this by the deliberate repetition of the word "simple" or the idea of simplicity. There are a great many examples in the book; here are a few:

- Lurie's simple solution to sex – paying Soraya: (p.1)
- Lurie's dinner with Melanie: *"It will be very simple."* (p.13)
- Lurie's response to Melanie's unresponsiveness after their intimacy: *"Don't make the situation more complicated than it need be."* (p.35)
- Lurie's response to the treatment of animals: *" ... if we are going to be kind, let it be out of simple generosity, not because we feel guilty or fear retribution."* (p.74)
- Even Lurie's complex opera of Byron and Teresa is pared down to very little. *"The lush arias he had dreamed of giving her he quietly abandons; from there it is but a short step to putting the instrument (the simple banjo) into her hands."* (p.184)
- In the end, Lurie gives up his little dog with a simple gesture of love: *"It will be little enough, less than little: nothing."* (p.220)

Language and Words

Definitions

- David Lurie is a teacher of communications, an expert on words. (as is Coetzee, see Author Information, p.79) Because there is nothing mightier than the word, Coetzee can be admired for his skill in wielding his pen so effectively.

- Coetzee plays with words at their simplest level: he starts with the root and then presents it in all its other possible forms. Through this deconstruction of language, he is able to show that ideas and perspective can shift by simply making the slightest change: in this case a letter or two. At times, the small changes are hardly noticed, but the overall effect can create a whole new meaning.

- **USURP, USURP UPON** - *"usurp upon means to intrude or encroach upon. Usurp, to take over entirely, is the perfective of usurp upon; usurping completes the act of usurping upon."* (p. 2) This applies to actions by both Lurie and Petrus.

- **COMPLIANT, PLIANT** - Soraya is described as a *"ready learner, compliant, pliant."* (p.5) Compliant refers to willing participation; pliant refers to being manipulated or influenced easily, either physically or emotionally. (Melanie, Lucy)

- **KIN, KIND** - Having been warned to *"Stay with [his] own kind"* (p.194), Lurie wonders about the conditions that create relations between strangers.

- **I LIVE, I HAVE LIVED, I LIVED** - As a communications teacher, Lurie is always trying to explain the subtle distinctions of word forms; for example, *"The perfective (verb form), [signifies] an action carried through to its conclusion. How far away it all seems."* (p.71) Life, as it was, has changed and is over.

- **DRINK, DRINK UP; BURNED, BURNT** (p.71) - The distinction between burned and burnt is simply one of degree. To be burned shows the action of having been burned; to be burnt shows the intense and finished state of having been burned. With the first, the object has undergone a change of state; with the second, the object is in the new, changed state. *"Everything is tender, everything is burned. Burned, burnt."* (p.97)

- It is interesting that Coetzee uses the actions of *"drinking and burning"* (p.71) in the same paragraph, because it foreshadows the attack on Lucy and Lurie. It is the use of methyl alcohol, a drinkable substance in another form, that is set on fire and burns David Lurie. A change of state applies not only to chemistry but to governments as well.

- Coetzee noticeably uses the present tense throughout the novel and, by doing so, traps our attention as readers. We only change perspective as Lurie changes perspective. In 1994, when the ANC assumed political control in South Africa, the situation was applauded and seemed settled. (see ANC, p.72) But, like Lurie, we slowly learn that things are not what they seem to be, nor have they yet become what they will be. The state of affairs in this novel, including all the characters, is in a present state of disgrace and needs urgently to be changed.

Other Languages

- Coetzee uses other languages, without the benefit of translation, to highlight the fact that there is always another, perhaps clearer, way of saying something. It may be clearer for the reader, but it doesn't seem to help the multilingual David Lurie:

    He speaks Italian, he speaks French, but Italian and French will not save him here in darkest Africa. (p.95)

Acronyms

- Coetzee uses acronyms, words formed from the first letters of other words, to create another level of meaning. *"On campus it is Rape Awareness Week. Women Against Rape, WAR, announces a twenty-four-hour vigil in solidarity with 'recent victims.'"* (p.43) Rape is a declaration of war on women and the emotions felt by women, who are victims of attack are just as raw as the emotions felt by those who perpetrate violence against them.

- Lurie is asked whether he has any *"objection to the presence of a student observer from the Coalition Against Discrimination?"* (p.48) The unofficial acronym of this committee (CAD) describes Lurie's behavior perfectly; he has indeed behaved like a cad.

Irony and Double Meanings

- Coetzee uses words to the utmost level of their power. He can create an ironic state of being or action with the single stroke of a word, or he can overlay ideas in a subtle manner.
- Lurie is so taken with Melanie at first that he imagines, for a fleeting instant, what it would be like to live with her.

    Every night she will be here; every night he can slip into her bed like this, slip into her. (p.27)

- Petrus, to Lucy and Lurie,

    "No more dogs. I am not any more the dog-man." (p.129)

- Petrus, to Lucy and Lurie, at his party:

    "Lucy is our benefactor," says Petrus; and then, to Lucy: *"You are our benefactor."* (p.129)

- In Lurie's opera about Byron, he describes Byron's abandonment of his daughter. Lurie imagines her to be *"dying of la mal'aria"* (and calling plaintively to her father) *"'Why have you forgotten me?'"* (p.186) In a similar way, Jesus appealed to his father, *"My God, why have you forsaken me?"*

- With the single word "mal'aria," Coetzee invokes not only the disease, malaria, which, translated from the original Italian, means "bad air," but he also creates the vision of an operatic actor singing badly about an important theme or idea. Coetzee is implying that there is something wrong with all the individual voices (in the opera and in the country) that we are listening to. (see Opera, p.60)

Parallels and Juxtaposition

- Each relationship and character in the novel has a parallel relationship or character to highlight the qualities Coetzee wants to emphasize or to juxtapose the qualities he wants to contrast.
    - Lurie and Soraya foreshadow Lurie's relationship with Melanie – the illustration of paid sex leads to Coetzee's portrayal of unpaid, unwanted sex (abuse) in the case of Melanie.
    - Melanie's experience with Lurie parallels and juxtaposes what later happens to Lucy – the abuse of Melanie foreshadows the rape of Lucy.
    - Lurie and Mr. Isaacs – both fathers of girls who have been sexually abused – both are looking for apologies.
    - Byron is as callous to Teresa as David Lurie is in his relationship with women in general.
    - Teresa is as plain and unloved as Lucy and Bev Shaw – here Coetzee is saying that everyone deserves to be loved.
    - The dogs and their fate in the novel – there are two incidents concerning dogs: first, when Lucy's dogs are murdered; second, in Bev's clinic where they are euthanized – each ends in death.
    - Lucy and Petrus – Lucy is Petrus's "master" and therefore his "protector"; this relationship turns around and Petrus becomes Lucy's "master and protector."

- Both Lurie and Petrus are parties to harassment and rape: one direct and the other indirect – at the same time, both consider themselves to be protectors.

- Through these parallels and juxtapositions, and through the use of the present tense, Coetzee leads us through the different levels of understanding and acceptance. He starts with minor relationships and situations (Soraya) and then presents escalating versions of the same idea. Each incident sets the reader up for the next more difficult and, finally, most horrible incident.

- All the parallels in the novel are merely representations of a bigger parallel to South Africa. He guides us to consider not the causes or the details of what has already happened, but to ponder the aftermath – what happens next? (see Dante, p.58)

SYMBOLS
Grace, Disgrace

South Africa

Dante

Dogs

Opera

SYMBOLS

Grace/Disgrace

- The theme of grace/disgrace can be shown on as many levels as it takes to define the words, grace/disgrace. The power of the single word, disgrace, stretches far. (see Keys, p.10) By using it as the title, Coetzee manages to convey an image, a description, an accusation, a blurring of the line between grace and disgrace, and finally, an acceptance.

- Coetzee introduces the idea of a religious state of grace. God automatically bestows grace on all living creatures. But, by their actions and free will, all living creatures are in danger of angering God and thus falling from grace. One way to reinstate oneself is to beg God's forgiveness.

- David Lurie is not a believer in God, but he finally realizes that he is being punished for what happened between himself and Melanie.

  I am sunk into a state of disgrace ... It is not a punishment I have refused ... On the contrary, I am living it out from day to day, trying to accept disgrace as my state of being. Is it enough for God, do you think, that I live in disgrace without term? (p.172)

- He prostrates himself in front of the Isaacs women. *"With careful ceremony he gets to his knees and touches his forehead to the floor."* (p.173)

- Coetzee also reinforces the idea of disgrace as shame. Lurie doesn't readily feel shame for his own actions, but later he does feel shame for what happens to Lucy. He takes Lucy's attack personally. *"Lucy's secret; his disgrace."* (p.109) He then tries to objectify it so that he can come to terms with the whole incident.

  Lucy, my dearest, why don't you want to tell? It was a crime. There is no shame in being the object of a crime. You did not choose to be the object. You are an innocent party. (p.111)

- Despite her innocence, Lucy feels the shame of her situation.

  She would rather hide her face [and not go to market] ... Because of the disgrace. Because of the shame. That is what their visitors have achieved; that is what they have done to this confident, modern young woman. Like a stain the story is spreading across the district. Not her story to spread but theirs ... (p.115)

- Even the dogs feel the shame of dying in an unnatural way.

    They flatten their ears, they droop their tails, as if they too feel the disgrace of dying; locking their legs, they have to be pulled or pushed or carried over the threshold. (p.143)

- There are many accusations of disgraceful conduct in the novel. People want to lay blame for many things, such as the immoral conduct of Lurie toward Melanie, Petrus's possible involvement in the attack on Lucy, the betrayal of the innocent dogs; but no one is sure how to begin. Accusations are thrown into the air just to see where they land and to see if some sense will come.

    (Rosalind): "I blame you and I blame her. The whole thing is disgraceful from beginning to end. Disgraceful and vulgar too. And I'm not sorry for saying so." (p.45)

- Although it is not a simple, clear-cut idea, the state between grace and disgrace is less confusing at the beginning of the novel than it is as the novel progresses. At the start, it is very clear that Melanie has suffered because of Lurie's abuse of power, and there appears to be little reaction.

    ... if he has been shamed, she is shamed too. But on Monday she reappears in class ... (p.31)

- But later when Lucy is raped, the emotions become conflicted and confused. Lucy has not yet come to understand that she has been attacked by the same people who were themselves victimized by apartheid policies.

    "It was so personal," [Lucy] says. "It was done with such personal hatred ... why did they hate me so? I had never set eyes on them."

    [Her father answers] "It was history speaking through them ... A history of wrong." (p.156)

- Everything has turned upside down. Suddenly Petrus is *"his own master"* (p.114) and Lucy is wanted *"for [his] slave."* (p.159) Lucy accepts her degradation, although Lurie argues with her. *"You wish to humble yourself before history. But the road you are following is the wrong one. It will strip you of all honour; you will not be able to live with yourself."* (p.160)

- Once the fall from grace has occurred, Coetzee believes that acceptance must be present in order to proceed to the future. He uses Nietzsche's idea that what doesn't kill us will make us stronger.

    Fallen? Yes, there has been a fall, no doubt about that...

    "Perhaps it does us good," (Lurie) says, "to have a fall every now and then. As long as we don't break." (p.167)

- The disgrace suffered by David Lurie, Lucy, the dogs, and South Africa's white community is pivotal. Although it has been shameful and humiliating, *"perhaps that is a good point to start from again."* (p.205) (see New Balance, p.35)

South Africa
The Country and the Policy of Apartheid

- South Africa is symbolized not only through the characters in the book, including David Lurie, Lucy, Melanie, and Soraya, but also by the incidents of rape and aggression. Because Coetzee has not used a single, unique symbol for South Africa, he is able to drive home his message to the reader through many avenues. His references are subtle and take on the air of questions tinged with a hint of accusation.

- Melanie's play, "Sunset at the Globe Salon," is a comedy set in the "new" South Africa, which portrays a gay hairdresser and a mixture of black and white clients. The play is a light caricature of the racism in the "old" South Africa. The presumption is that everything can simply be "washed away" and thus changed.

  > *Patter passes among the three of them: jokes, insults. Catharsis seems to be the presiding principle: all the coarse old prejudices brought into the light of day and washed away in gales of laughter.* (p.23)

- Coetzee uses Melanie as a victim, like South Africa's victimized blacks, to show the need for change.

  > *She is behaving badly, getting away with too much; she is learning to exploit him and will probably exploit him further. But if she has got away with much, he has got away with more; if she is behaving badly, he has behaved worse. To the extent that they are together, if they are together, he is the one who leads, she the one who follows. Let him not forget that.* (p.28)

- When Lurie signs the document of complaint against him, his signature goes alongside that of Melanie, his accuser. This signifies the beginning of the process of legal division between these two, just as the whites and the blacks signed their documents signifying the beginning of the legal process to end apartheid.

  > *The deed is done. Two names on the page, his and hers, side by side. Two in a bed, lovers no longer but foes.* (p.40)

- Later in the novel, we see that the situation, in both the lives of the characters and in the country, is bad. Lucy is raped; positions of hierarchy have been reversed; life has been literally turned upside down. After the attack on Lucy, she accepts that this may be the price for remaining *"on their territory"* and she considers whether *"that is the price one has to pay for staying on."* (p.158)

- Lurie's teaching of Wordsworth's poem, "The Prelude," is an indirect reference to the reality and ideology of apartheid. Lurie has tried to live his life under the illusion that he could compartmentalize people and things. The pure idea of compartmentalization is a basis for the policy of apartheid. In referring to this poem, Coetzee questions the coexistence of ideology and reality. He is alluding to the necessity for a new balance. (see New Balance, p.35)

    ... we cannot live our daily lives in a realm of pure ideas, cocooned from sense-experience. The question is not, How can we keep the imagination pure, protected from the onslaughts of reality? The question has to be, Can we find a way for the two to coexist?

    The passage is difficult ... Nevertheless, Wordsworth seems to be feeling his way toward a balance: not the pure idea ... but the sense image ... (p.22)

- The struggle for independence for the blacks has not been a one-sided one. Many whites were very active and supportive in the quest to end apartheid, but they now feel they no longer know their place. (see Apartheid, p.71; Shift of Power, p.32) When Lurie watches the very successful finished presentation of Melanie's play, he sits uneasily in the audience.

    Though they are his countrymen, he could not feel more alien among them, more of an impostor. Yet when they laugh at Melanie's lines he cannot resist a flush of pride. Mine! he would like to say .... (p.191)

- To further aggravate the situation, Lurie is accosted by Melanie's boyfriend, Ryan, who tells him, *"Stay with your own kind ... Find yourself another life, prof. Believe me."* (p.194) But Lurie does not know how to do this. He has lost his job; his daughter has lost her farm; he no longer knows who is in charge.
- Things have changed in a very short time.

   Between Lucy's generation and mine a curtain seems to have fallen. I didn't even notice when it fell. (p.210)

Notice how Coetzee uses the single word "curtain" as a metaphor which can refer simultaneously to a boundary between stage and audience, between generations and its individuals, or between one stage in life and another; it can also mean "the end."

- The novel reaches a point where change can no longer be postponed. Change must begin somewhere, and for Coetzee it must begin with a fresh perspective. For Lucy, change means that Petrus will now own her property.

   ... perhaps that is a good point to start from again ... To start at ground level. With nothing. Not with nothing but. With nothing. No cards, no weapons, no property, no rights, no dignity. (p.205)

- If Nietzsche is right, then whatever does not kill them will serve to make them stronger. (p.191) While Lurie may feel he is *"too old to heed, too old to change"* (p.209) his life, he finally understands that he must, although it may be humiliating. But even as he is unsettled with the present unease and instability, he tells himself that *"... it does not have to last for ever. Nothing has to last for ever."* (p.211)

- New situations or balances must be tried before they become true and workable. Coetzee believes the important thing is to try.

Dante *Guided Change*

- Coetzee continues to emphasize that change need not be done in a vacuum. To this end, he uses Dante's poem, "The Divine Comedy of Dante Alighieri" as a metaphor for guided change. Dante is taken on a guided tour through the three areas of Hell, Purgatory, and Paradise. It is the change from one realm to another that concerns Coetzee. He wants to show that the transition from the old order in South Africa to the new one after apartheid may be very difficult.

    > *[Bev Shaw guides the animals from life to death.] I don't think we are ready to die, any of us, not without being escorted.* (p.84)

    > *[Lurie contemplates the change in his professional life.] So much for the poets, so much for the dead masters. Who have not, he must say, guided him well.* (p.179)

- By using Dante, Coetzee alludes to Lurie's/South Africa's descent into chaos and hell. Both have fallen into a state of disgrace.

    > *An image comes to him from the Inferno: the great marsh of Styx, with souls boiling up in it like mushrooms ... Souls overcome with anger, gnawing at each other. A punishment fitted to the crime.* (p.209, 210)

Dogs *Animal Rights Symbolizing Human Rights*

- Lurie tells Lucy the story of a golden retriever who became out of control whenever he was sexually aroused. The owners would beat him, and eventually the dog reacted to his own sexual drive by behaving as if he really had been beaten.

> *One can punish a dog ... for an offense like chewing a slipper. A dog will accept the justice of that: a beating for a chewing. But desire is another story. No animal will accept the justice of being punished for following its instincts.* (p.90)

- This story is a subtle analogy to Lurie's justification for his own sexual behavior – *"I became a servant of Eros"* (p.52) – and a further analogy to the blacks of South Africa reacting to being beaten down for wanting to control their own destiny.

- Brilliantly, Coetzee follows this scene by immediately portraying the rape of Lucy, which represents the violent consequence of a long and complicated history. *"She shortens the Dobermanns' leashes. The men are upon them."* (p.91)

- In addition, Bev Shaw and her clinic play a significant role in this discussion. It is here that the ideas of dignity and disgrace over the treatment of animals (humans) are played out, each clarifying the other. Bev's Animal Welfare League no longer receives government funding and she does her work out of love for the animals. *"On the list of the nation's priorities, animals (blacks) come nowhere."* (p.73)

- Lucy also emphasizes the idea that the policy of apartheid is unnatural. By placing animals and humans side by side on the scale of life, she points to the juxtaposed existence of blacks and whites. *" ... there is no higher life. This is the only life there is. Which we share with animals. "* (p.74)

- But her father is not convinced. He still believes there is an innate difference between blacks and whites, and thus, he is exempt from the obligation to create a different order.

  > *As for animals, by all means let us be kind to them. But let us not lose perspective. We are of a different order of creation from the animals. Not higher, necessarily, just different.* (p.74)

- But as Lurie becomes more involved with the dogs, his feelings begin to change.

    One Sunday evening ... he actually has to stop at the roadside to recover himself. Tears flow down his face that he cannot stop. He does not understand what is happening to him. Until now he has been more or less indifferent to animals. Although in an abstract way he disapproves of cruelty, he cannot tell whether by nature he is cruel or kind. He is simply nothing. (p. 142, 143)

Opera   As a Symbol of Balance

- Opera is based on human dialogue in musical form and must blend the many elements of voice, music, story line and characterization. The idea of an opera about Byron and his lover, Teresa, helps Coetzee make an analogy to South Africa. He uses the operatic form as a perfect symbol for showing that a country must balance successfully the needs and voices of all its citizens. Its importance in the novel is illustrated by the fact that Coetzee devotes an entire section, pages 180 through 186, to the discussion of Lurie's attempted work of art.

- Coetzee takes the reader through Lurie's labored creative process. Lurie's original conception for Byron and Teresa needed to have characters who would *"balance one another well: the trapped couple, the discarded mistress ... the right mix of timelessness and decay."* (p.180, 181) In the end it is the victim, Teresa, and not the controlling force, Byron, who cries out to be heard. (see Literary Allusion, p.65)

- It is clear that Coetzee, like Lurie, is trying to find a way for the multiple voices of the country to blend together; but, like Lurie, he comes to the conclusion that a single voice is the one that must be heard without interference from other sound sources. The "music" no longer suits either community and the two *"will demand a music of their own."* (p.183)

- Coetzee has followed through on his premise of simplicity. The novel itself is slightly more than two hundred pages, a lightweight in the novel world. He has used deconstructed language (see Language, p.42) to refine his themes, but the simplest technique he uses is to write this story as if it were being played in two acts: the before and the after. The curtain of the first act comes down when Lucy and Lurie see the men on the road. *"The men are upon them."* (p.91)

- The use of the play and opera structures are interchangeable. While Melanie is performing in a play about the changing South Africa, Lurie is attempting to write an opera about Byron and the changes in his life. Meanwhile, Melanie, Lucy and Lurie all are dealing with the traumatic changes in their own lives.

- In both art forms (play and opera) the narration is removed and only the characters are present to communicate directly with the audience. In a sense, Coetzee's narration in the novel is also minimal; he lets the actions speak for themselves.

- The five-page attack scene (p.93-97) is made more powerful by its lack of descriptive and lurid detail. The climax of this attack is described in a single paragraph in the centre of this scene. (p.95) With simple sentences, bare of adjectives and adverbs, Coetzee delivers the coup de grace.

    Now the tall man appears from around the front, carrying the rifle ... There is a heavy report; blood and brains splatter the cage. For a moment the barking ceases. The man fires twice more. (p.95)

- Because music and poetry (both of which are contained in opera) are a means to reach the human soul, the opera format is the one that Coetzee (Lurie) uses to explore the issue of divergent perspectives, different needs, and different solutions. (Note that Lurie also teaches poetry.) Coetzee, through David Lurie, simplifies the answer by coming to the conclusion that the virtually unknown Teresa, and not the famous Byron, should be alone on stage.

- Although Teresa (clearly a symbol for the ravaged South Africa) is a *"dumpy little widow"* who is *"past her prime,"* Lurie wonders

    Can he find it in his heart to love this plain, ordinary woman? Can he love her enough to write a music for her? If he cannot, what is left for him? (p.181, 182)

- When Lurie realizes that his main character, Byron, has given way to the needs of Teresa, he changes the perspective of the opera. Teresa's point of view now takes precedence. By placing her on a stage with a simple banjo as accompaniment at the end of the play, Lurie gives her the place and space to allow her voice to be heard. In the analogy, the black community's voice, now unaccompanied, is the one that simply must be heard.

LAST THOUGHTS
Literary, Historical Allusions
Lord Byron, Teresa

LAST THOUGHTS

Literary and Historical Allusions

- Perhaps it is not accidental that many of Coetzee's literary references – Dante (see p.58), Dostoevsky, Descartes, Drood, Dreyfus – all begin with the letter "d." In the hands of Coetzee, master linguist, it must surely be intentional. These references stand out to remind us of the other "d" words, despair and disgrace.

- Dostoevsky (1821-1881), the great Russian writer, was arrested in 1849, along with other members of the literary elite. He was jailed as a dangerous criminal and subjected to a fake execution, where a firing squad, with unloaded rifles, aimed at him and fired. This was how his sentence was commuted before he was exiled from Russia, not allowed to return until 1859. His great novel, **Crime and Punishment**, written in 1866, dealt with an alienated hero, Raskolnikov, who was resentful of the controlling forces that were contributing to the moral disorder and decay of his society. (Bradbury) The entire novel, **Disgrace**, is permeated with echoes of Dostoevsky's concern with the paradigm of crime and punishment.

- Descartes (1596-1650) is famous for *Cogito, ergo sum*: I think, therefore I am, which implies that we are first and foremost thinking beings, and everything else comes after that. In contemplating Petrus's sheep, Lurie thinks of the ignominy of their destiny – to be eaten and used, with only the gall bladder remaining. There is nothing graceful about that. This organ is named for a state of irritability. Coetzee thinks about those other "sheep" (the blacks) who have been led to the slaughter.

  Nothing escapes, except perhaps the gall bladder, which no one will eat. Descartes should have thought of that. The soul, suspended in the dark, bitter gall, hiding. (p.124)

- **The Mystery of Edwin Drood** was Charles Dickens's (1812-1870) last, unfinished novel about the young Edwin Drood, who is allegedly murdered. He disappeared, as did the outcome of his story, since Dickens died before his book was finished. Lucy is reading this book (p.76) prior to the rape, and Lurie notices its absence after the rape. Petrus is also mysteriously absent in the days following the rape. These small references are significant for what goes missing: people, ideas, a future plan.

  Of Edwin Drood there is no more sign. (p.114)

- Alfred Dreyfus (1859-1935) was a captain in the French military who was accused of being a spy for Germany, the enemy of France. The accusation against him was based on circumstantial evidence, but he was nevertheless found guilty, court-martialed and exiled to Devil's Island. Emile Zola, the French novelist, became interested in the case and published an open letter denouncing the army's involvement. This letter re-opened the case against Dreyfus. His famous "J'accuse!" (I accuse!) is the reference here and is echoed in the accusation that Melanie's father makes against Lurie.

> *There, points the nicotine-stained finger of (Melanie's) father. The hand slows, settles, makes its X, its cross of righteousness: J'accuse.* (p.40)

- As described in his autobiography, **Boyhood**, Coetzee was witness to the merciless beating of a colored servant. (see Dogs, p.58) He could relate to the fear of the servant, because Coetzee himself feared being beaten by his teachers. He imagined that one day the servant would want to get even.

- So began his fascination with the difference between the tortured and the torturer, an idea that presents itself in all of Coetzee's novels. Both find themselves in a state of disgrace and, eventually, a decision must be made on how to disengage oneself from such a state of being. One way is through violence, another, through deliberation and debate.

Lord Byron and Teresa

- Lord Byron, the poet, was born George Gordon Noel Byron in 1788 and died in 1824. He was married to Anne Isabella Milbanke and, in 1815, had one child with her. When they separated in 1816, Byron left for Italy, never to return to England.

- He was very promiscuous and purportedly had an affair with his half-sister. When he met Countess Teresa Guicciolo, in April of 1819, she was only nineteen years old and married to a man nearly three times her age. Byron fell madly in love with her and followed her everywhere, including to Ravenna. (p.87, 121, 180, etc.)

- He became an integral part of her family and was very close to her father and brother, who were political revolutionaries. When they were eventually exiled for their activities, they left Ravenna and found asylum in Pisa. Byron followed them to Pisa and so was able to continue his involvement with Teresa. This period of Byron's life lasted about two years, during which he was artistically prolific and produced some of his best work.

- During this time, Byron was friends with Percy Bysshe Shelley and his wife, the writer Mary Shelley, and they spent much time discussing Wordsworth's poetry (which Lurie teaches) and telling ghost stories. These activities gave Mary Shelley the idea for her novel, **Frankenstein**.

- After about two years with Teresa, Byron again became bored and restless. He left Pisa in 1823 and went to help the Greeks in their attempt to overthrow the Turkish rulers of the day. He felt he would die in Greece, and in 1824 he succumbed to a fever that ended his life. Although Byron had left Britain in disgrace (the breakup of his marriage was a scandal at the time) and was not allowed to be buried in Westminster Abbey, he continues to be honored in Greece for his revolutionary efforts on that country's behalf.

HISTORICAL REFERENCES

Apartheid, ANC

Truth/Reconciliation Commission

Population, Demographics

HISTORICAL REFERENCES

Apartheid

- Apartheid is literally translated as "apartness": the state of being apart. After the 1948 general election in South Africa, Daniel F. Malan, the leader of the Afrikaner Nationalist Party (NP), established the official policy of segregating the blacks and reinforcing the supremacy of the whites. The official policy also separated different groups of nonwhites from each other, including various groups of Africans.

- According to the Columbia Encyclopedia, groups of black Africans and other nonwhites were removed against their will from their homes and transferred to townships outside the urban centers as early as 1950. Approximately one and a half million Africans were displaced in the years between 1950 and 1986. Separate "homelands" were established for the different ethnic groups. They were not allowed to own land or vote, and they had to carry passes at all times.

- The international community began to take notice of South African racial and ethnic policies and enforced international economic sanctions, which had a devastating effect on the nonwhite population. Widespread local opposition to apartheid in the 1970s and 1980s, along with the sanctions, resulted in the slackening of some of the segregationist laws and policies. The last laws were repealed in 1991 by President F. W. de Klerk. The first open election resulted in a victory for Nelson Mandela and the African National Congress.

African National Congress (ANC)

- The ANC was originally formed in 1912 by tribal chiefs and the heads of various religious groups. Its main purpose was to stand united against oppression and to promote the rights of the African people. Its main focus was nonviolent resistance. In the 1940s and 1950s it became connected to Indian, coloured, and liberal white groups that supported civil disobedience, which the members of the ANC hoped would result in political freedom. Instead, the ANC was banned, and the activists continued their struggle in a more aggressive way. In 1963 some of the ANC leaders, including Nelson Mandela and Walter Sisulu, were arrested, tried, and imprisoned. Nelson Mandela received a life sentence but was released in 1990.

Truth and Reconciliation Commission

- One of the first truth commissions ever held was in Uganda in 1974. Others followed in Argentina, Chile, Haiti, Rwanda, just to name a few countries. The purpose of truth commissions is to explore past human rights violations without seeking blame and retribution.

- Mr. Dullah Omar, a former Minister of Justice in South Africa, said this about the establishment of a truth and reconciliation commission: *"... a commission is a necessary exercise to enable South Africans to come to terms with their past on a morally acceptable basis and to advance the cause of reconciliation."* (TRC Home Page)

- In 1994, Nelson Mandela's newly elected government set up a multiracial committee empowered to research and document the range of human rights abuses in South Africa between 1960 and 1994.

- South Africa's Truth and Reconciliation Commission was headed by Archbishop Desmond Tutu and consisted of three components: **amnesty** (to guarantee that the perpetrators of political crimes would be free to speak), **human rights violations** (to investigate the crimes of abuse and identify the victims), and **reparations and rehabilitation** (to provide support for the victims, to restore their dignity, and to recommend the future course of healing for everyone). The commission could investigate and identify criminal behavior but had no power to pursue criminal activity.

- One of the commission's most famous investigations concerned Nelson Mandela's former wife, Winnie Madikizela-Mandela, who had been implicated and convicted in a sensational case of the kidnapping, assault, and murder of a 14-year-old boy, Stompei Seipei Moketsi. In 1991, her six-year prison sentence was reduced to a fine. In 1997, Madikizela-Mandela testified before the commission and was judged to have been aware of and to have encouraged the activities that led to Stompei's death.

- When the committee released its final report in October 1998, it concluded that the government had committed grievous human rights abuses. Furthermore, it specifically named P. W. Botha, former Prime Minister; Mangosuthu Buthelezi, the leader of the Inkatha Freedom Party; Winnie Madikizela-Mandela, and others who were politically active in the dreadful events of the time.

Population - Demographics

- In 1950, when apartheid was first established, the government had no official census procedures in place, but intended to take a population count at the beginning of each new decade. Numbers were difficult to come by because there were millions of people, mostly blacks, who lived in "squatter camps" and so were unaccounted for. Squatter camps were filled with transient people who worked or who hoped to work in nearby cities. Regardless of the lack of numbers, the blacks were restricted to geographic areas comprising only 13 percent of the total area of South Africa. In 1994, the Mandela government set the population of South Africa at approximately 40.4 million people. To the best of their knowledge, the population demographics were as follows: 76.4 percent black, 12.6 percent white, 8.5 percent coloured, and 2.5 percent Asian. Government estimations at present predict that by the year 2025, the population of South Africa will have doubled. (The term "coloured" is written according to the British spelling rules which are used in South Africa.)

Coloured

- South AFrica's coloured population included several million people of mixed-race status, who were distinctly not all black, all Asian, or all white. Most of these people speak Afrikaans as their main language and live in the west and north of the country; only a small percentage of the coloureds speak mainly English. The largest subgroup live just north of Cape Town and are members of the Dutch Reformed Church. Another sizeable subgroup of coloureds are descendants of Afrikaners, mixed with the indigenous Khoikhoi and slaves brought to South Africa from the Dutch East Indies. They are a separate community because they are mostly Muslim.

- The coloureds, under apartheid, were also forced to change homes and neighborhoods. While they did not have the same rights as whites, they did have political rights that the blacks did not have. For example, they were allowed to vote in elections, but only for the coloured representatives. They used this right to try to improve their own lot in life and to fight apartheid.

Afrikaners and Others of European Descent

- Afrikaners make up about 7 percent of the population of South Africa and are people who descend from the Dutch, German, Belgian and French settlers. They had come to the southern part of Africa as early as the seventeenth century, in part to escape religious oppression; but then, ironically, they became the oppressors in their new homeland. They fought the British for control in the now famous Boer War (1905) and lost. However, in 1910, a unified South Africa was established with Afrikaans, a variation of Dutch, as an official African language. It stands beside English as a language of literature and many works are first written in Afrikaans then translated into English, such as the work of the novelist André Brink.

- There is also a small community of English speakers who are descended mainly from the British that includes Jews who came from Britain or Eastern Europe. This community was, for the most part, not supportive of apartheid policy.

Asians

- There are about one million people who are mostly of Indian descent. These people were originally brought to South Africa as agricultural workers, but this practice ended in about 1913 because the South African government closed the door to immigration from India. They speak English as a first language but may also speak Tamil or Hindi. Despite the persecution they endured, they did become successful businessmen, teachers, and artisans. Like the coloured population, the Asians had rights, separate from the rights of the white community.

AUTHOR INFORMATION

AUTHOR INFORMATION

- John Maxwell Coetzee, like Peter Carey (author of **Oscar and Lucinda, True History of the Kelly Gang**), is a two-time winner of the Booker prize for literature. His first winning novel was **The Life and Times of Michael K** (1983); the second was **Disgrace** (1999). In choosing the book, the committee felt that **Disgrace** is not just a book about South Africa in post-colonial times, but about the shift of power throughout the world away from Western control.

- Born in 1940, Coetzee grew up in Cape Town, South Africa, in an English-speaking family of Afrikaner background. In his autobiography, **Boyhood**, Coetzee talks about his distant relationship with his alcoholic father and the almost stifling closeness of his mother. Coetzee's family was a part of the middle class, which found themselves struggling after the war. This struggle is evident in his memoir, with Coetzee referring to himself only in the third person. In this way, he tries to contain the pain and torment of his unhappy childhood.

- Like his fellow South African writers, Nadine Gordimer, Alan Paton, Athol Fugard, and André Brink, Coetzee is a dedicated observer of the history and politics of South Africa. He is fascinated by the fact that the psychology of a country is the same as the psychology of the people it imprisons – isolating and self-hating – so he looks at the relationship between the prisoner and the prison-keepers. He explores the concept of how people in authority can behave inhumanely to those under their control. He is disturbed by the number of political activists like Steven Biko who died by "suicide" in 1977 while in police custody. By writing about the inhumane conditions in which these activists found themselves, Coetzee hopes to effect change.

- In a 1986 article for The *New York Times*, Coetzee wrote:

  Let us be clear about the situation of the prisoner who falls under suspicion of a crime against the state. What happens in Vorster Square (a prison) is nominally illegal. Articles of the law forbid the police from exercising violence upon the bodies of detainees except in self-defense. But other articles of law, invoking reasons of state, place a protective ring around the activities of the security police.

- Coetzee has often been compared and contrasted to Nadine Gordimer. While both address their love for their country and the challenges of the seemingly unsolvable juxtaposition of white and black society within that country, each views it from a different standpoint. Gordimer weaves history into her fiction; Coetzee leaves out the actual history but uses it to create an atmosphere for his stories. He feels that " ... *history is not reality* ... *history is a kind of discourse*" **("The Novel Today")**; in other words, history is something to be discussed in a novel. Coetzee does not want to be controlled by the history because history is based on an agreed-upon perspective of what has occurred. When there are different perspectives, the "discourse" has to change.

- J.M. Coetzee holds a master's degree in the work of Ford Madox Ford and a doctorate in the work of Samuel Beckett. His early education included training in computer science and linguistics. He has spent his professional time teaching literature at the University of Cape Town, the University of Chicago and Stanford University. In 2002, Coetzee emigrated to Australia and holds an honorary position at the University of Adelaide.

Other Works by J. M. Coetzee

FICTION

Dusklands
In the Heart of the Country
The Master of Petersburg
Age of Iron
The Life and Times of Michael K
Foe
Waiting for the Barbarians
Disgrace
Elizabeth Costello
Slow Man

NON-FICTION

White Writing
The Lives of Animals
Giving Offense
Boyhood: Scenes from
    a Provincial Life
Youth
Stranger Shores
Doubling the Point:
    Essays and Interviews

PRIZES

The Booker Prize (1983) **The Life and Times of Michael K**

The Booker Prize (1999) **Disgrace**

The Nobel Prize in Literature, 2003

FROM THE NOVEL
Quotes

FROM THE NOVEL ...

Memorable Quotes from the Text of Disgrace

PAGE 3. Although he devotes hours of each day to his new discipline, he finds its first premise, as enunciated in the Communications 101 handbook, preposterous: "Human society has created language in order that we may communicate our thoughts, feelings and intentions to each other." His own opinion, which he does not air, is that the origins of speech lie in song, and the origins of song in the need to fill out with sound the over large and rather empty human soul. (Lurie)

PAGE 4, 5. Because he has no respect for the material he teaches, he makes no impression on his students ... He continues to teach because it provides him with a livelihood; also because it teaches him humility, brings it home to him who he is in the world. The irony does not escape him: that the one who comes to teach learns the keenest of lessons, while those who come to learn learn nothing. (Lurie)

PAGE 16. ... a woman's beauty does not belong to her alone. It is part of the bounty she brings into the world. She has a duty to share it. (Lurie)

PAGE 31. What happened to his car was evidently not enough. Evidently there are more installments to come. What can he do? He must grit his teeth and pay, what else? (Lurie)

PAGE 33. Note that we are not asked to condemn this being with the mad heart, this being with whom there is something constitutionally wrong. On the contrary, we are invited to understand and sympathize. But there is a limit to sympathy. (Lurie, on the teaching of Byron)

PAGE 44. Don't expect sympathy from me, David, and don't expect sympathy from anyone else either. No sympathy, no mercy, not in this day and age. Everyone's hand will be against you, and why not? Really, how *could* you? (Rosalind to Lurie)

PAGE 56. "Are you sorry?" says the girl. The recorder is thrust closer.

"Do you regret what you did"

"No," he says. "I was enriched by the experience"

... "So would you do it again?"

"I don't think I will have another chance."

"But if you had a chance?" ... "Ask him if he apologized," someone calls to the girl.

Confessions, apologies: why this thirst for abasement?

PAGE 62, 63. "I have plans. Something on the last years of Byron. Not a book ... Something for the stage, rather. Words and music. Characters talking and singing."

"I didn't know you still had ambitions in that direction."

"I thought I would indulge myself. But there is more to it than that. One wants to leave something behind. Or at least a man wants to leave something behind. It's easier for a woman."

"Why is it easier for a woman?"

"Easier, I mean, to produce something with a life of its own." (Lurie talking with Lucy)

PAGE 71. So: a new adventure. His daughter, whom once upon a time he used to drive to school and ballet class, to the circus and the skating rink, is taking him on an outing, showing him life, showing him this other, unfamiliar world. (Lurie at the market)

PAGE 79. "Forgive me, Lucy," he says ... "For being one of the two mortals assigned to usher you into the world and for not turning out to be a better guide."

PAGE 95. He is helpless, an Aunt Sally, a figure from a cartoon, a missionary in cassock and topi waiting with clasped hands and upcast eyes while the savages jaw away in their own lingo preparatory to plunging him into their boiling cauldron. Mission work: what has it left behind, that huge enterprise of upliftment? Nothing that he can see. (Lurie/attack)

PAGE 98. A risk to own anything: a car, a pair of shoes, a packet of cigarettes. Not enough to go around, not enough cars, shoes, cigarettes. Too many people, too few things. What there is must go into circulation, so that everyone can have a chance to be happy for a day. That is the theory; hold to the theory and to the comforts of theory. Not human evil, just a vast circulatory system, to whose workings pity and terror are irrelevant. That is how one must see life in this country: in its schematic aspect. Otherwise one could go mad.

PAGE 110. I don't know whether insurance policies cover massacres. I will have to find out. (Lucy)

PAGE 112. Vengeance is like a fire. The more it devours, the hungrier it gets. (Lurie to Lucy)

PAGE 117. He would not mind hearing Petrus's story one day. But preferably not reduced to English. More and more he is convinced that English is an unfit medium for the truth of South Africa.

PAGE 133. Don't shout at me, David. This is my life. I am the one who has to live here. What happened to me is my business, mine alone, not yours, and if there is one right I have it is the right not to be put on trial like this, not to have to justify myself – not to you, not to anyone else. As for Petrus, he is not some hired labourer whom I can sack because in my opinion he is mixed up with the wrong people. That's all gone, gone with the wind. (Lucy)

PAGE 141. He has recovered the sight of his eye completely. His scalp is healing over; he need no longer use the oily dressing ... So time does indeed heal all.

PAGE 151. Against this new Petrus what chance does Lucy stand? ... Were this a chess game, he would say that Lucy has been outplayed on all fronts. If she had any sense she would quit: approach the Land Bank, work out a deal, consign the farm to Petrus, return to civilization.

PAGE 197. Is it his earth too? It does not feel like his earth. Despite the time he has spent here, it feels like a foreign land. (Lurie going back to visit Lucy)

PAGE 199. What kind of child can seed like that give life to, seed driven into the woman not in love but in hatred, mixed chaotically, meant to soil her, to mark her, like a dog's urine?

PAGE 206. At once the dog is upon him (Pollux) ... Swine! Never has he felt such elemental rage. He would like to give the boy what he deserves: a sound thrashing. Phrases that all his life he has avoided seem suddenly just and right: Teach him a lesson, Show him his place. So this is what it is like, he thinks! This is what it is like to be a savage! (Lurie)

PAGE 207. Falling to her knees, Lucy grips the dog's collar, speaking softly and urgently .... "Are you all right?" she says.

The boy is moaning with pain. Snot is running from his nostrils. "I will kill you!" he heaves .... "We will kill you all!" he shouts.

ACKNOWLEDGEMENTS

ACKNOWLEDGEMENTS

Bradbury, Malcolm, general editor. *The Atlas of Literature*. Stewart, Tabori & Chang, New York. 1998.

Coetzee, J.M. "The Novel Today." *Weekly Mail*, 1987.

Coetzee, J.M. "Into the Dark Chamber: The Novelist and South Africa." The *New York Times*, Jan. 12, 1986.

South Africa, Country Guide: www.1upinfo.com

Stein, Jess (editor-in-chief). *The Random House Dictionary*, unabridged. Random House, New York. 1966.

Truth and Reconciliation Commission Home Page: www.doj.gov.za/trc